The Magic Porridge Pot

Retold by Rosie Dickins

Illustrated by Mike and Carl Gordon

Reading Consultant: Alison Kelly
Roehampton University

This story is
about hungry
Hannah,

an old
woman,

a greedy
boy,

a magic
pot

and a LOT of porridge.

3

Hannah never had
enough to eat.

But, when she had some
food, she always shared it.

One day, Hannah
found some honey
in the forest.

Mmm,
honey...

Then she saw an old
woman. The woman was
carrying an empty pot.

"Would you like some
honey?" asked Hannah.

9

"Yes please," said
the old woman.

"Would you like some porridge?"

11

"I'd LOVE some porridge,"
said Hannah.

"But your
pot is empty."

The woman smiled. "That doesn't matter," she said. "You just need to know the magic words."

Cook pot, cook!

Hot porridge filled the pot.

Stop pot, stop!

Then it stopped.

Hannah and the woman
ate a delicious meal of
porridge and honey.

“You can keep the pot,” said the woman.

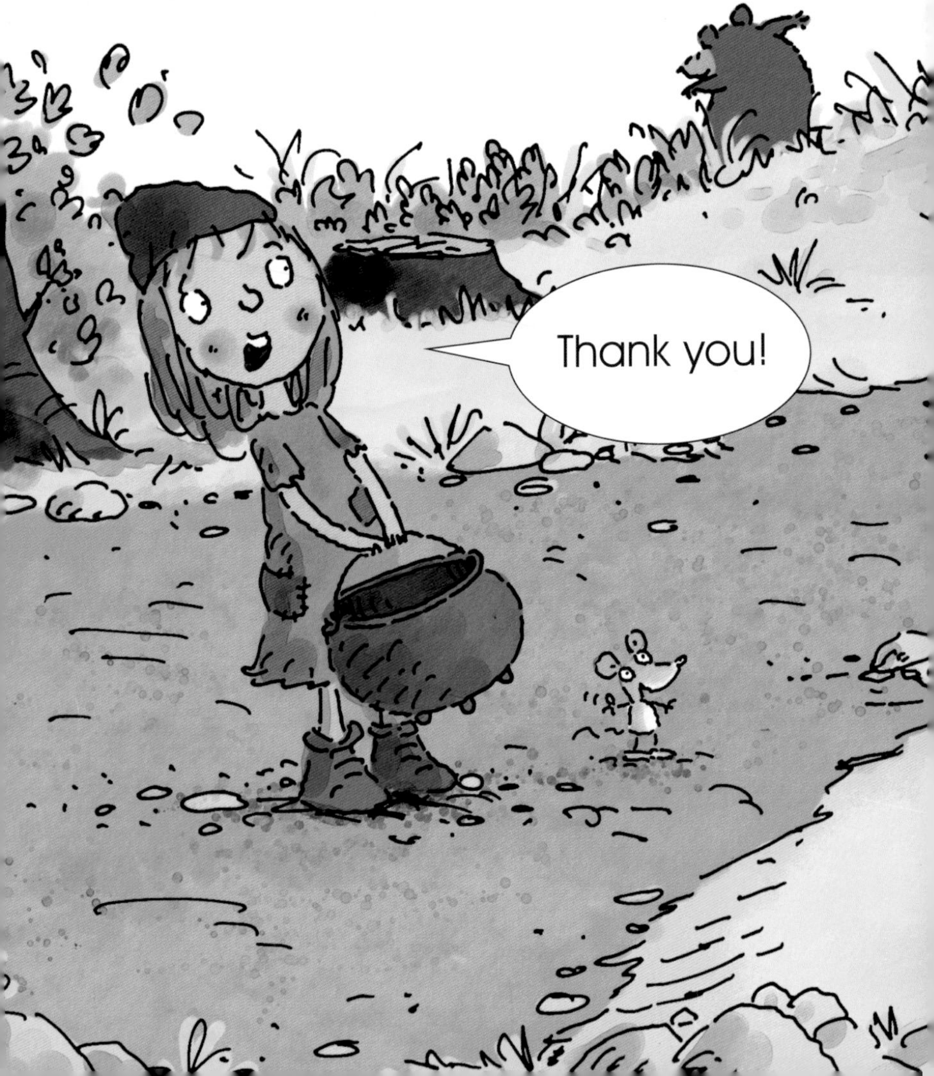

"Remember the magic
words and you will never
be hungry again."

21

From then on, Hannah
always had plenty to eat.

She had porridge for
breakfast...

porridge for lunch...

and porridge for dinner.

One evening, a greedy
boy smelled the porridge.

He followed his nose
to Hannah's cottage.

He saw the pot start to
fill with porridge...

...but he didn't see it stop.

The boy waited until
Hannah went to bed.

Then he crept in, stole the pot and ran home.

He couldn't wait to say
the magic words...

cook pot, cook!

Steaming porridge
filled the pot.

Porridge dripped over
the sides.

"Stop!" cried the boy.
But the pot didn't stop.

Porridge poured
onto the floor.

"Stop!" cried the boy.
But the pot didn't stop.

Porridge filled the room.

"Stop!" cried the boy. But the pot didn't stop.

The boy ran outside.

"Stop!" cried the boy.
"I'll drown in porridge!"

But the pot didn't stop.

In her bedroom, Hannah sniffed. "I smell porridge!" she thought.

She ran outside.

Oh no! It must
be the pot.

Porridge was pouring
down the street.

Hannah shouted
the magic words.

Stop pot, stop!

And at last, the
pot stopped.

The greedy boy was saved.

But he had to eat a lot
of porridge before he
could go home.

45

As for Hannah...

she got her pot back, and
no one ever stole it again.

About this story

The Magic Porridge Pot is based on a traditional tale from Europe. People have been telling different versions of the story for centuries. It was first written down 200 years ago, by the brothers Jacob and Wilhelm Grimm. They called it *Sweet Porridge*.

Series editor: Lesley Sims

Designed by Zoe Waring

First published in 2007 by Usborne Publishing Ltd., Usborne House,
83-85 Saffron Hill, London EC1N 8RT, England. www.usborne.com
Copyright © 2007 Usborne Publishing Ltd.